I CAN READ IT ALL BY MYSELF

Beginner Books

January

February

March

April

May

June

July

August

September

illustrated by *Art Cumings*

BEGINNER BOOKS   A Division of Random House, Inc.

October

November

December

Please Try to Remember the FIRST of OCTEMBER!

OCTEMBER

By Dr. Seuss*

*writing as Theo. LeSieg

www.seussville.com

Library of Congress Cataloging-in-Publication Data:
Seuss, Dr.   Please try to remember the first of Octember!   "B63."
SUMMARY: Every wish is fulfilled on the First of Octember.
[1. Wishes—Fiction.   2. Stories in rhyme]   I. Cumings, Art.   II. Title.
PZ8.3.G276P1   [E]   77-4504
ISBN: 0-394-83563-8 (trade) ; ISBN: 0-394-93563-2 (lib. bdg.)

Printed in the United States of America   17

BEGINNER BOOKS, RANDOM HOUSE, and the Random House colophon are registered
trademarks of Random House, Inc.

Everyone wants
a big green kangaroo.

Maybe, perhaps,
you would like
to have TWO.

I want you to have them.
I'll buy them for you . . .

. . . if you'll wait
till the First of October.

Everyone wants

a new skateboard TV.

Some people want two.

And some people want three.

Perhaps you want four?

Well, that's O.K. with me . . .

. . . if you'll wait

till the First of Octember.

Just say what you want.

You want pickles on trees?

Want to swing
through the air
on a flying trapeze?

Just say what you want,
and whatever you say,
you'll get
on Octember the First.

WHAT
A
DAY!

When October comes round,
you can play a hot tune
on your very expensive
new Jook-a-ma-Zoon!

I wish you could play it

in May or in June.

But May is too early.

And June is too soon.

When October gets here,
no work! And no school!

We'll build you a playhouse!
We'll build you a pool!
We would build them
right now,
but right now
is too cool.

And we'll buy you
a wonderful
Jeep-a-Fly kite!

We will!
If you'll wait
till the month is just right.

Octember's the best
because March is too dusty.
And April won't do
because April's too gusty.

What <u>more</u> do you want?

Do you and your dog
want more time to relax? . . .
Less time on your feet
and more time on your backs? . . .
More time in the air
and less time on the ground? . . .

You'll get it
as soon as
October comes round.

Want to take a great trip?
Well, I know a great ship.

It sails
to Alaska,
Nebraska and Sweden,
making stops
in Ga-Dopps
and the Garden of Eden.

And it sails on the First of Octember!

What <u>else</u> do you want?

Want to play a new sport?

In October
we'll build you
a Hock-Zocker court!

You'll get all that you want.

You just write out your list.

Everyone has an October First list

Write slowly now!
Don't break your wrist.

Then one of these days
the October First van
will drive up to your house
just as fast as it can.

Whatever you want,
you will get in big bags,
and boxes and crates
with your name on the tags.

You'll have
rockets to shoot.

You'll have
bombs you can burst . . .

. . . on the wonderful
night of

OCTEMBER
THE
FIRST!

On the First of Octember
you'll stay up all night,
drinking 66 six-packs
of Doodle Delight.

Whatever
you ask for,
I want
you to get.

But October—
I'm sorry—
just isn't <u>here</u> yet.

SO ...
Be sure
to be here.
Be sure you're in town
on Octember the First ...

. . . when
the
money
comes
down!

It doesn't
come down much
in March
or November—
or even September . . .

. . . or in August,

October,

July

or December.

But
EVERYTHING'S
YOURS . . .

. . . on the First
of Octember!

On the First
of Octember?

Thank <u>you</u>!
I'll remember.

DR. SEUSS (who was known as Theodor Geisel when he wasn't writing or drawing) wrote and illustrated 44 books for children and their lucky parents. But sometimes Dr. Seuss liked to write books and have someone else draw the pictures. For those books he used the pen name Theo. LeSieg (which is Geisel spelled backward!). To draw the pictures for this book, he chose…

ART CUMINGS, who was a cartoonist and magazine illustrator for many years. When his three sons were young, Mr. Cumings decided to start illustrating books for children. He especially enjoyed working on this book since it gave him the chance to work with one of his favorite writers.

Millions of Americans remember Dick and Jane (and Sally and Spot too!). The little stories with their simple vocabulary words and warmly rendered illustrations were a hallmark of American education in the 1950s and 1960s.

But the first Dick and Jane stories actually appeared much earlier—in the Scott Foresman Elson Basic Reader Pre-Primer, copyright 1930. These books featured short, upbeat, and highly readable stories for children. The pages were filled with colorful characters and large, easy-to-read Century Schoolbook typeface. There were fun adventures around every corner of Dick and Jane's world.

Generations of American children learned to read with Dick and Jane, and many still cherish the memory of reading the simple stories on their own. Today, Pearson Scott Foresman remains committed to helping all children learn to read—and love to read. As part of Pearson Education, the world's largest educational publisher, Pearson Scott Foresman is honored to reissue these classic Dick and Jane stories, with Grosset & Dunlap, a division of Penguin Young Readers Group. Reading has always been at the heart of everything we do, and we sincerely hope that reading is an important part of your life too.

Library of Congress Cataloging-in-Publication Data is available.

ISBN 0-448-43400-8 (pbk)   B C D E F G H I J
ISBN 0-448-43412-1 (GB)   B C D E F G H I J

Read with
Dick and Jane

We Look

GROSSET & DUNLAP • NEW YORK

Look

Look, look.

Oh, oh, oh.

Oh, oh.
Oh, look.

Jane

Oh, Jane.

Look, Jane, look.

Look, look.

Oh, look.

See Jane.

See, see.

See Jane.

Oh, see Jane.

Dick

Look, Jane.
Look, look.
See Dick.

See, see.
Oh, see.
See Dick.

Oh, see Dick.

Oh, oh, oh.

Funny, funny Dick.

Sally

Look, Dick.
Look, Jane.
See Sally.

Oh, oh, oh.

Oh, Dick.

See Sally.

Look, Jane.

Look, Dick.

See funny Sally.

Funny, funny Sally.

Big and Little

Come, come.

Come and see.

See Father and Mother.

Father is big.

Mother is little.

Look, Father.
Dick is big.
Sally is little.
Big, big Dick.
Little Baby Sally.

Oh, look, Jane.

Look, Dick, look.

Sally is big.

Tim is little.

Big, big Sally.

Little Baby Tim.

The Funny Baby

Come down, Dick.

Come and see.

See the big, big mother.

See the funny little baby.

Puff is my baby.

Puff is my funny little baby.

I see the big mother.
I see the little baby.
Look, Jane.
See the big father.

Look, Dick, look.

See something funny.

See my baby jump.

See my baby run.

Oh, oh, oh.

Something Blue

Oh, Jane, I see something.
I see something blue.
Come and see Mother work.
Mother can make something.
Something blue.

Look Mother, look.

I can work.

I can make something.

I can make something yellow.

Look, look.

See something yellow.

Oh, Jane, I can work.

I can make something blue.

I can make something yellow.

Oh, see my funny Tim.

Little Tim is yellow.

Baby Sally is blue.